Published 1984 by
The Hamlyn Publishing Group Limited
London . New York . Sydney . Toronto
Astronaut House, Feltham, Middlesex, England

©Editiones Peralt Montagut 1984

ISBN 0 600 30820 0
Printed in Italy

Instead, he asked her where
she was going.

'Oh, I am going to see my grandmamma and give her these cakes,' said Little Red Riding-Hood.

'Does she live far away?' asked the wolf.

'She lives
on the other side
of the wood –
near the mill.'

'Oh,' said the wolf
thinking hard. 'Well,
I'm afraid I'm not
going that way
so I'll say
goodbye.'

And the wolf ran off through the trees.

Little Red Riding-Hood
went on her way, gathering
nuts and picking flowers
as she went.

The cunning wolf went straight
to the grandmother's house and
tapped on the door.

'Who's there?' called Little Red Riding-Hood's grandmother.

'It's Little Red Riding-Hood,' answered the wolf in a high voice.

'Come in dear,' said grandmamma from her bed.

As soon as the wolf was inside,
he ate up the old lady.
He put on her nightdress
and frilly bonnet,

closed the door,

and jumped into the bed.

When Little Red Riding-Hood
arrived, she knocked at the door.

'Who's there?'
came a strange,
gruff voice.

'Grandmamma must have a very bad cold,' thought Little Red Riding-Hood. 'Her voice sounds quite hoarse.'

But she said, 'It's me, Little Red Riding-Hood. I've brought you some of Mummy's nice cakes.'

'Come straight in my dear,' called the wolf.

When Red Riding-Hood went in, the wolf hid
under the bedclothes and said
to her, 'Put the cakes on
the table and come and
give me a big
kiss.'

As soon as Little Red Riding-Hood got close to
the bed she saw how strange her
grandmother looked.
'Grandmamma, what big arms you have!' she said.
'All the better to hug you with my dear,'
said the wolf.

'Grandmamma what big ears
you have!'

'All the better to hear you with my dear.'

'Grandmamma, what big eyes you have!'

'All the better to see you with my dear.'

'Grandmamma what big teeth you have!'
'All the better to eat you with, my dear.'

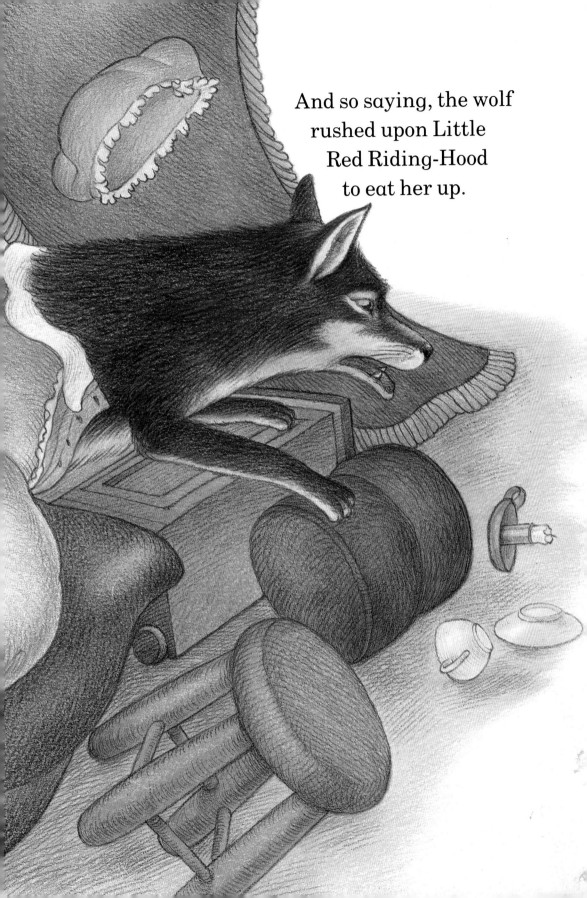

And so saying, the wolf
rushed upon Little
Red Riding-Hood
to eat her up.

Fortunately, a hunter was passing and,
hearing the commotion, he rushed in
and saved Little Red Riding-Hood.

He killed the wolf and opened
him up, and out jumped the
old grandmother.

Everyone was very pleased. The
huntsman took home a fine wolf's skin, and
Grandmamma ate the delicious cakes
for her tea.

Little Red Riding-Hood promised she would
be more careful when she walked through the
wood, and would never talk to a wolf again.